MOUSE SHAPES

a very first book

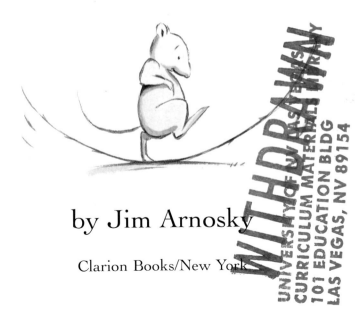

by Jim Arnosky

Clarion Books/New York

For Martin, to share with Freya

Clarion Books
a Houghton Mifflin Company imprint
215 Park Avenue South, New York, NY 10003
Copyright © 2001 by Jim Arnosky

The illustrations were executed in brush and ink with an acrylic wash.

www.houghtonmifflinbooks.com

Printed in Singapore.

Library of Congress Cataloging-in-Publication Data
Arnosky, Jim.
Mouse shapes : a very first book / by Jim Arnosky.
p.   cm.
Summary: A mouse scrambles through an obstacle course,
introducing the reader to simple shapes.
ISBN 0-618-01522-1
[1. Mice—Fiction. 2. Shape. 3. Stories without words.] I. Title.
PZ7.A7384 Mop 2001
[E]—dc21

TWP   10 9 8 7 6 5 4 3 2 1

CIRCLE

OVAL

TRIANGLE

SQUARE

DIAMOND

RECTANGLE

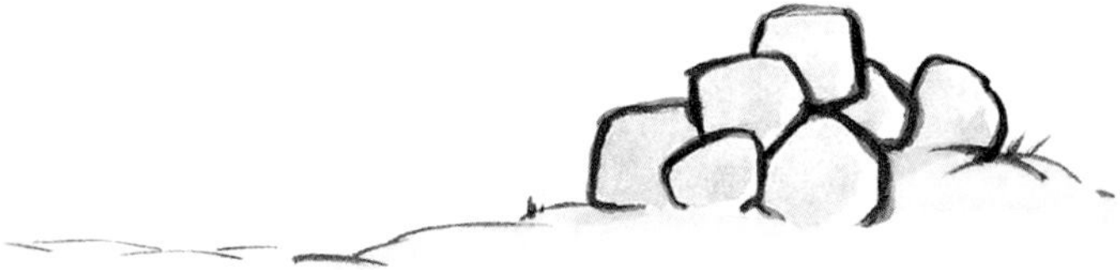

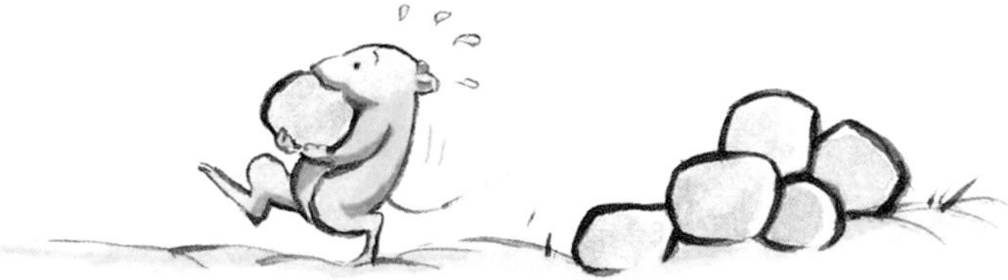

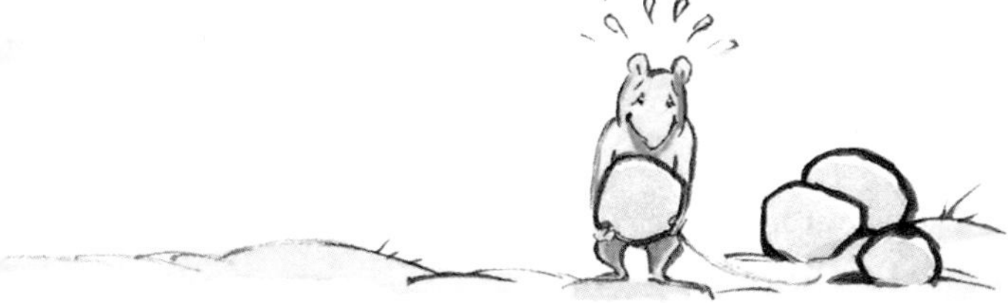

PARALLEL

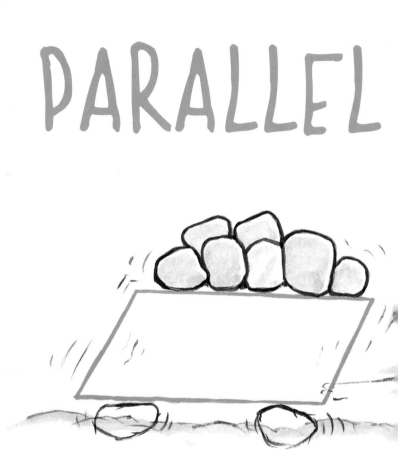

OGRAM

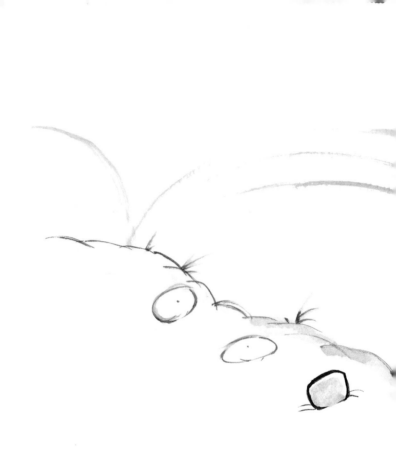

TRAPEZOID

PENTAGON

HEXAGON